W9-BQS-767

AMAZING MINIFIGURE
ULTIMATE STICKER COLLECTION

How to use this book

Read the captions, then find
the sticker that best fits the space.
(Hint: check the sticker labels for clues!)

•

Don't forget that your stickers can
be stuck down and peeled off again.

•

There are lots of fantastic extra stickers too!

LONDON, NEW YORK,
MELBOURNE, MUNICH, AND DELHI

Written and edited by Emma Grange
Designed by Anne Sharples
Cover designed by Lauren Rosier and Lisa Sodeau

Published in the United States
in 2013 by DK Publishing
375 Hudson Street, New York, New York 10014

10 9 8 7 6 5 4 3 2 1

001–187857–Jan/13

Page design copyright © 2013 Dorling Kindersley Limited

A CIP catalog record for this book is available from the Library of Congress.

ISBN: 978-1-4654-0173-1

Printed and bound by L-Rex, China

Discover more at
www.dk.com
www.LEGO.com

IN THE FOREST

It is always busy in the land of LEGO® City. The forest is full of dangers, so the police and the firefighters have lots of work to do. There are robbers on the run and forest fires to put out—and bears to avoid!

Swamp Crook
This crook is escaping across the forest swamp on a discarded crate. After him!

Air Police
The police often use helicopters to search for criminals in the woods. They wear special flight vests to keep them safe.

Forest Police
The Police Ranger tracks down criminals hiding in the forest. He uses a flashlight and a radio to help him.

Forest Firefighter
All the trees in the forest are a fire hazard! If a fire starts, firefighters are soon on the scene with fire extinguishers and hosepipes.

Forest Crook
This robber is getting away! Is he planning a burglary with this crowbar?

Help the police and fire brigade save the day by using your extra stickers on this page . . .

THERE'S A GRRR-EAT VIEW FROM UP HERE! GRR!

BATTLES

The LEGO® Kingdoms are at war. The Dragon Kingdom has invaded the Lion Kingdom and captured the Lion Princess! Royal knights and soldiers ride out from both kingdoms to do battle. Who will win this fight of good versus evil?

Lion King
The Lion King rules the Lion Kingdom wisely. He will fight to protect his land—he will not let it be conquered!

Lion Queen
The Lion Queen rules alongside the King. She likes to watch jousting competitions.

Blacksmith
Lots of knights means a lot of armor and weapons. The local Blacksmith is on hand to forge new swords and shields.

Elite Dragon Knight
Beware—this fierce knight fights only for the Dragon Kingdom. At heart he is just a big bully.

Royal Lion Knight
To the rescue! The Royal Lion Knight is the bravest of all the knights. He will ride out to fight for his kingdom—and to free the princess.

©2013 LEGO

Lion Princess

The Lion Princess is a damsel in distress. She trusts that the Lion Knights will come to save her.

Dragon Wizard

The stern Dragon Wizard is a mysterious character. Watch out or he'll turn you into a toad, or worse!

©2013 LEGO

©2013 LEGO

HAHA! TAKE THAT, YOU PUNY DRAGON KNIGHT!

Court Jester

The Jester makes silly jokes and wears a silly costume. Unfortunately, not everyone finds him funny.

Obi-Wan Kenobi™

Obi-Wan Kenobi is a brave Jedi. He persuades the Jedi Council to train Anakin and becomes his Jedi Master.

Count Dooku™

Count Dooku left the Jedi to join the Sith. He follows orders from Darth Sidious, even fighting against Anakin and Obi-Wan.

Ahsoka Tano™

Ahsoka is from the planet Shili. She is a Jedi Padawan under Anakin's training, and is eager to prove herself.

Darth Vader™

When Anakin falls to the dark side, he becomes the Sith Lord Darth Vader. He turns against the Jedi, including his former friends.

Senator Palpatine™

The power-hungry politician Palpatine is secretly the Sith Lord Darth Sidious! He persuades Anakin to join the dark side.

Darth Maul™

Darth Maul is the apprentice of the Sith Lord Darth Sidious. He fights fiercely with a double-bladed lightsaber.

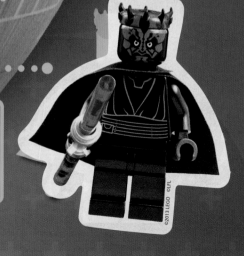

SPACE SAGA

Trouble is brewing in the LEGO® *Star Wars*® galaxy. The evil Sith have returned, seeking to seize power with the dark side of the Force. The Jedi must fight back to restore peace. Come and meet some of the weird and wonderful people, aliens, and creatures involved in this galactic battle.

Yoda™
Yoda is the wisest, and oldest, Jedi of them all. He leads the Jedi High Council and is strong in the light side of the Force.

Anakin Skywalker™
Anakin is a young Jedi Knight. He struggles to control his emotions and is tempted by the dark side of the Force.

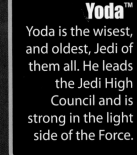

Boba Fett™
Boba Fett is a clone. He is hunting for revenge after his father, Jango Fett, was destroyed by a Jedi in a fight.

Jar Jar Binks™
Jar Jar is a Gungan from the swamps of Naboo. He is very clumsy and is always getting into trouble! Whoops!

Luke and Leia Skywalker™
Twins Luke and Leia were raised separately, not knowing that Anakin was their father. They both fight against the dark side during the Galactic Civil War.

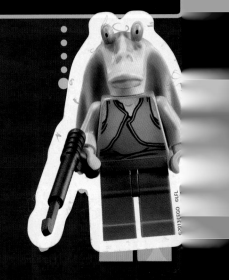

A GREAT ADVENTURE

Welcome to Middle-earth! In the peaceful land of the Shire, a Hobbit called Frodo Baggins is visited by a Wizard and embarks on an epic journey. Frodo must destroy the powerful One Ring before the Dark Lord Sauron finds it. He is soon helped on his way by a group called The Fellowship of the Ring. Join them in the realm of LEGO® *The Lord of the Rings*™.

Gandalf the Grey™
Gandalf the Grey is the oldest and wisest Wizard in Middle-earth. He uses his knowledge and magic to fight evil. He knows he must resist the power of the One Ring.

Frodo™ Baggins
The young Hobbit Frodo has never been outside the Shire before! He may be small, but he has been given a big and important task . . .

Samwise Gamgee™
Sam is Frodo's best friend and gardener. He hopes that one day people will tell stories about how brave he was when he helped Frodo save Middle-earth.

Aragorn™
Aragorn helps to lead the Fellowship on their way through Middle-earth. He will fight bravely to the very end to ensure Frodo destroys the One Ring.

Gimli™
Gimli the Dwarf loves a good battle. He makes up for his short temper and short stature with his strength and skill with the ax.

Moria™ Orc

This nasty creature is an Orc from the murky Mines of Moria. The Orcs are angry when disturbed by The Fellowship of the Ring!

Merry and Pippin

Troublemaking twosome Merry and Pippin are Frodo's cousins. They often get into trouble, but are kind and funny—and always hungry.

Legolas™

Elves are peaceful creatures, but Legolas vows to fight for Middle-earth. His speed and agility with a bow and arrow come in handy in a fight.

Ringwraith™

This dark shadowy figure is a Ringwraith. Ringwraiths can sense the power of the One Ring and are bound to obey the Dark Lord Sauron.

Boromir™

Boromir tries to seize the One Ring for himself. But he soon realizes that friendship is more important, and helps the Hobbits in a fight against the Orcs.

ANCIENT QUEST

Professor Hale is an archaeologist on a mission. He is leading an intrepid expedition hunting for Pharaoh Amset-Ra's long-lost treasures. But Hale and the LEGO® Pharaoh's Quest team must battle evil mummies and booby-trapped pyramids to find the treasure before Amset-Ra returns!

Professor Archibald Hale
Professor Hale swapped his dusty books for the sandy desert. Now he carries a map and a pickax, and is far from the safety of his library!

Jake Raines
Pilot and daredevil Jake Raines loves adventure. Coming face-to-face with flying mummy warriors might change his mind!

Helena Skvalling
Helena is the best of the best when it comes to hunting for long-lost treasures. She and Jake used to be rivals but have united to stop Amset-Ra.

Mac Mcloud
Clumsy mechanic Mac Mcloud is always stumbling into trouble. Luckily he has the technical skills to speed his team to safety again!

Amset-Ra
Pharaoh Amset-Ra is about to reawaken! By combining all his treasures he would have the power to take over the world.

Flying Mummy

What's more frightening than a mummy warrior? A flying mummy, of course! These bandaged warriors can swoop down on the Pharaoh's lost treasures.

I SPHINX I CAN FLY FASTER THAN YOU, MUMMY!

©2013 LEGO

©2013 LEGO

©2013 LEGO

Mummy Warrior

These mummy warriors serve Amset-Ra. They look scary, but are easily tricked by clever adventurers.

Anubis Guard

The fierce Anubis Guards protect the Scorpion Pyramid where Amset-Ra is buried. They wear the jackal-headed masks of the Egyptian god Anubis.

DANGEROUS DINOS

Uh-oh! The LEGO® Dino dinosaurs have broken out of their compound! Here come the five brave Dino Hunters, trying to track down and capture these colossal creatures. They will catch as many dinosaurs as they can before returning to the safety of their Dino Defense HQ.

Rex Tyrone
Rex Tyrone once caught 20 dinosaurs in one day! He is happy to race after Raptors all day long.

Josh Thunder
Josh Thunder is the leader of the Dino Strike Team. He stays connected to the other Dino Hunters at all times.

Sue Montana
Sue is the only girl on the Dino Hunter team. She once caught as many dinosaurs as Rex Tyrone.

Tracer Tops
Tracer Tops is a terrific tracker! He is also very skilled with a tranquilizer gun.

Chuck "Stego" Jenkins
Chuck is a slightly nervous Dino Hunter. He would prefer to be taking photographs, or back at HQ, eating sandwiches!

A MAGICAL WORLD

Welcome to the world of LEGO® Harry Potter™!
When Harry Potter was just a baby, he survived an
attack from the evil Lord Voldemort™. Eventually, with
the help of his friends, Harry defeats Voldemort in
a thrilling battle—preventing the Dark Lord and his
followers from taking control of the wizarding world.

Hermione Granger™

Although she initially
appears too competitive
and studious for Harry
and Ron, Hermione
proves to be a loyal
and trustworthy friend.

Ron Weasley™

Ron and Harry become
friends when they meet
on the Hogwarts Express.
They are both sorted into
Gryffindor house.

Neville Longbottom™

Neville Longbottom
is a good-natured,
accident-prone
wizard who is
forever misplacing
his toad, Trevor!

Luna Lovegood™

A quirky Ravenclaw
student, but loyal to
the end, Luna tells
Harry about the
Thestrals that pull
the school carriages.

Dobby™

Dobby the house-elf
first visits Harry at
number four, Privet
Drive. He tries to keep
Harry from returning
to Hogwarts.

Lord Voldemort

The evil Lord Voldemort is
called "You-Know-Who" by
most witches and wizards,
as they are too terrified
to speak his name.

SAIL THE SEAS

Captain Jack Sparrow is off on another swashbuckling adventure on the stormy seas. This infamous pirate sails onboard his beloved ship *The Black Pearl*, seeking excitement and treasure. Meet the LEGO® *Pirates of the Caribbean*™: a motley bunch of unusual friends, crew, and fearsome, undead foes.

Captain Jack Sparrow
Many tales have been told about the legendary Captain Jack—most of them exaggerated or made up!

Elizabeth Swann
Elizabeth is the headstrong daughter of Governor Swann. She takes on pirates and grave peril to be with her beloved Will.

Angelica
No one knows for sure, but Angelica is said to be Blackbeard's daughter. She can match her old friend Jack in a fight—and is dressed like him too!

William Turner
Blacksmith William Turner starts out hating pirates. But after his adventures, he comes to see that a pirate's life might not be so bad.

Davy Jones
Davy Jones captains *The Flying Dutchman*. He has a terrifying temper, and an equally scary undead crew!

Bill Turner
"Bootstrap" Bill Turner is William Turner's long-lost father. He is a part of Davy Jones' undead crew.

Hector Barbossa

Barbossa was once Captain Jack Sparrow's friend—until he led a mutiny and seized control of *The Black Pearl*.

Joshamee Gibbs

The faithful Gibbs is Jack's old first mate. He is often called upon to help rescue Jack, but would rather be relaxing on a beach!

Syrena

The beautiful mermaid Syrena was captured by Blackbeard. Rare mermaid tears can be used in a potion for eternal life.

Blackbeard

The infamous pirate Edward Teach is better known as "Blackbeard." He is just as mean as he looks and sounds.

Hadras

This undead pirate has been a part of Davy Jones' crew so long he looks like a hermit crab. He is guarding the chest containing Davy Jones' heart.

MONSTER MAYHEM

Watch out! Monsters have overrun the Earth! This beastly bunch is on a hunt to collect all seven magical Moon Stones so that they can rule the Earth forever. Thankfully, Doctor Rodney Rathbone has built a team of LEGO® Monster Fighters to fight back and find the stones first.

Doctor Rathbone
Aristocrat Dr. Rodney Rathbone leads the Monster Fighters. He has a false leg—perhaps the result of a fight with a monster!

The Vampyres
Lord and Lady Vampyre rule over all the monsters. They only come out at night and have a wicked plan to plunge the whole world into darkness.

Frank Rock and Ann Lee
These two are tough and trained to fight. Monsters should quake with fear at the sight of them—they have located a Moon Stone.

WOOOOO!

Werewolf
Avoid this monster when there is a full moon! The Werewolf has long sharp teeth and claws for biting and scratching.

Swamp Monster

The gruesomely green Swamp Creature lurks in the spooky swamplands. This scaly fiend once stole Frank Rock's pet dog!

Zombies

Don't disturb this deadly duo! The Zombie Bride and Groom prowl the graveyard and will eat anything in their path.

Ghost

It's behind you! The ghoulish ghosts love to sneak up on unsuspecting people and scare them.

The Crazy Scientist

Look out! The Crazy Scientist has created a monstrous monster to follow his evil instructions. Together they are mad, bad, and dangerous.

Mummy

This cursed creature is undead and very unfriendly. The Mummy is a mean monster who doesn't mind who he attacks.

©2013 LEGO

HEROES VS. VILLAINS

Yikes! Gotham City and Metropolis are under threat from rogues rising up around them. The streets are full of crime, but help is at hand. Meet some very special LEGO® DC Universe™ Super Heroes— and the villains that they have to fight on a daily basis to keep their cities safe . . .

Batman™

Bruce Wayne is Batman, also known as the Dark Knight or the Caped Crusader—the protector of Gotham City. He fights to rid the streets of crime.

Superman™

Clark Kent is the super-strong hero Superman, or the Man of Steel. He is always ready to fly to the rescue of his city, Metropolis.

Aquaman

The heroic Aquaman rules the seas. He also fights on land alongside Batman, Superman, and Wonder Woman.

Wonder Woman

Diana Prince is Wonder Woman—an Amazon warrior with amazing superpowers. Foes should think twice about taking her on in a fight!

Commissioner Gordon

There are not many people who Batman trusts. Commissioner Gordon, from the Gotham City Police Department, is a true ally in his fight against crime.

Bane

Bane is violent and dangerous. Batman knows that this fierce foe is not just super-strong, but super-intelligent, too.

Mr. Freeze

Brrr! This is one cool customer. Mr. Freeze is a cold-hearted criminal who likes to blast his enemies with ice.

The Joker

This clownish criminal is the Caped Crusader's archenemy. He is always up to no good, and loves plotting villainous crimes.

Lex Luthor

Brainy billionaire Lex Luthor is Superman's evil enemy. He loves creating new technology to try to take over Metropolis.

Catwoman

This cat-like villain is hard to predict. Sometimes Catwoman works with Batman, and sometimes she just wants to get her claws on stolen gems.

21

A LAND OF LEGEND

The ancient land of LEGO® Ninjago is a mystical place, filled with magical weapons and powerful forces. But it is also threatened by evil. The wise Sensei Wu has trained four brave Ninja to protect the world and battle against the sneaky Skeleton Army and the slithering Snakes. NINJA-GO!

Sensei Wu

Sensei Wu trains the Ninja in the art of Spinjitzu. He helps them to master the power of their Elements and unlock their full potential.

Cole

Cole is the black Ninja of Earth. He is the leader of the four Ninja and is brave and determined.

Kai

Kai is the red Ninja of Fire. He can be hot-headed, but his new robes show he has reached the highest level of Ninja training.

Jay

Jay is the blue Ninja of Lightning. Blink and you might miss him—he can move at supersonic speeds!

Zane

Zane is the white Ninja of Ice and is also a robot. He is always cool, calm, and collected.

Nya

Kai's younger sister, Nya, wants to be a Ninja, too. She trains hard to become the strong and powerful Samurai X.

Lloyd Garmadon

Young Lloyd turns from his rebellious ways to become the Green Ninja. Now he has to fight one last battle: against his father, Lord Garmadon!

Pythor

This s-s-sinister purple Snake is Pythor, the leader of the Serpentine. He is mean and horrible, and the sole survivor of the tribe of Anacondrai.

Samukai

Samukai is the sneaky General leader of the Skulkins. He leads the Skeleton Army and the Underworld by force.

Lord Garmadon

Sensei Wu's evil brother Lord Garmadon rose from the Underworld with four arms and great power. Now he can wield four weapons at once!

©2013 LEGO

23

ALIEN ATTACK

LEGO® Alien Conquest aliens are invading Earth! These extra-nasty extraterrestrials are searching for human brains to power the batteries on their spaceships. It is up to the astronauts in the Alien Defense Unit (ADU) to fight off this threat to the planet and save the day.

ADU Sergeant
The serious ADU Sergeant will see any job done. He is in charge of ridding Earth of the alien invaders.

ADU Soldier
It might be too late for this ADU Soldier—an alien Clinger has latched onto her head to steal all of her brainpower.

Alien Commander
The mean and green Alien Commander is determined to cause chaos. He wants human brainpower and he wants it now!

Alien Trooper
An Alien Trooper will shoot his laser gun first and ask questions later. They are not the smartest, which is why they want human brains, not alien brains!

Alien Pilot
The Alien Pilot uses fresh brainpower to charge his galactic batteries. Now he can fly his spaceship at supersonic speeds.

Make your own out-of-this-world scene by sticking your extra stickers on this page . . .

ACTION!

The toys in Andy's toy box are alive! Little does he know, but his playthings are often off on adventures more amazing than his wildest dreams. Woody, Buzz, and their fantastic plastic LEGO® Toy Story™ friends are often dodging danger, having fun, and even avoiding being thrown out in the trash.

Buzz Lightyear
To start with, Buzz Lightyear had trouble believing he was just a toy. He thought he really could fly—to infinity and beyond!

Sheriff Woody
Woody is Andy's oldest and favorite toy. At first he did not trust the newcomer Buzz Lightyear, but now the two are best buddies.

GREAT WEST

$

Jessie

Jessie the yodeling cowgirl loves fun and adventure. She has a soft spot for Buzz.

Green Army Man

The Green Army Men are good at following orders. They keep a lookout for humans approaching.

Zurg

The evil Emperor Zurg battles with Buzz before revealing that he is Buzz's father! Zurg believes he really did come from outer space.

Stinky Pete

Stinky Pete is an enemy of Woody's. A long way away from the Wild West, Pete is permanently bad-tempered.

Alien

The tiny three-eyed Aliens are eternally grateful to Andy's toys for rescuing them from the grabber machine.

Lotso

Don't be fooled by the friendly appearance of this fluffy pink bear— Lotso is actually a mean-spirited toy.

IN THE CITY

Come and meet some of the many people who live and work in the LEGO® City! The City is a busy, bustling place, kept safe and peaceful thanks to the hardworking police and firefighters. No crime goes unnoticed—especially with agents like Chase McCain on the case!

Chase McCain

Chase McCain is an agent in the City police force. He is ace at tracking and catching rotten robbers and not-so-crafty crooks.

Fire Chief

The Fire Chief has a very important job—he is in charge of the whole fire department! He wears a special golden helmet.

Businesswoman

This businesswoman works hard. She loves her job, so is always smiling!

Mechanic

When the businesswoman's car breaks down, this mechanic is on hand to change a tire.

City Crook

This crook is trying to make off with a wheelbarrow full of stolen gems. He won't get far with the police hot on his tail!

Truck Driver

This City worker drives a massive truck full of fuel. It is his job to deliver it safely to the fuel station.

Road Worker

The roads in the City are very busy and sometimes need repair. This worker is helping to make the road as good as new.

Cat Owner

This lady is very grateful to the firefighters—they rescued her cat when it got stuck up a tree!

Firefighter

When she is not putting out flames, this firefighter enjoys playing fetch with her pet dog in the park!

OH DEAR— IT'S A BIT HIGH UP HERE!

FIRE 600

MARVELOUS MINIFIGURES

You might find this amazing selection of LEGO® Series 8 Minifigures at the theater, under the sea, up a mountain, or even at a rodeo. Can you work out who they are? Which is your favorite?

Actor
To be or not to be—that is the question. This actor takes his role very seriously, with the costume and props to match.

Lederhosen Guy
This German guy is wearing national clothes—lederhosen. He is snacking on his favorite food—a pretzel. Wunderbar!

American Football Player
The American Football Player has used his tackling talents to win a trophy! His protective gear lets him knock opponents out of the way.

Female Skier
Take to the slopes! The Female Skier is wrapped up warm and equipped to ski down snowy mountainsides.

Cheerleader
The cheerful cheerleader looks excited. Maybe she is supporting the trophy-winning American Football Player.

Cowgirl
The Cowgirl is ready to lasso any rogue cows that run away. Round them up, Cowgirl!

Diver
The Diver is dressed for deep-sea diving. He wears a helmet and carries a harpoon.

Fairy
The Fairy wears wings and waves a wand. She grants wishes with a sprinkling of fairy dust.

Robot
This evil Robot has been built with wacky weapons and is programmed to follow truly dastardly instructions. Watch out!

MMMM! PRETZELS— MY FAVORITE!

DISGUSTING HUMAN FOOD!

©2013 LEGO

LEGENDS OF CHIMA

The Kingdom of Chima used to be a land of peace and friendship. But now the many animal tribes that live there have turned against one another. All of them are fighting for control of the powerful Chi orbs. Unleash the power of LEGO® Legends of Chima!

Laval
Laval finds it hard to choose between being a responsible ruler and having fun. This prince of the Lion Tribe still has lots to learn.

Cragger
Competitive Crocodile Cragger wants to win at everything. He used to be Laval's best friend, but now seeks Chi and power more than anything else.

Razar
Keep an eye on your possessions, or Razar will fly off with them! Ravens are selfish, and Razar will steal anything he can get his hooked claw on.

Winzar and Wakz
These wolves distrust all other tribes. They may pretend to be nice, but will be secretly plotting behind everyone else's backs.

Eris
Most of the Eagle Tribe have their heads in the clouds, but Eris is different. She loves stories and solving puzzles.

©2013 LEGO